HISTORY OF THE CIVIL RIGHTS MOVEMENT

Coloring Book

STEVEN JAMES PETRUCCIO

DOVER PUBLICATIONS, INC.
Mineola, New York

Introduction

The civil rights movement was the largest social movement of the twentieth century, influencing the modern women's rights movement and the student movement of the 1960s. The goal of the civil rights movement was to achieve equal opportunities for the basic privileges and rights of U.S. citizenship for African Americans. The roots of the drive for civil rights go back to the nineteenth century, but the movement was especially active in the 1950s and 1960s. African-American men and women, along with their supporters, organized and led the movement at national and local levels, using the law, petitions, and nonviolent protest demonstrations. This book highlights significant events in the civil rights movement in the United States, an important chapter in the nation's history.

The civil rights movement centered on the American South, where the African-American population was concentrated and where racial inequality in education, jobs, politics, and the law were commonplace. Beginning in the late nineteenth century, state and local governments passed segregation laws, known popularly as "Jim Crow" laws, as well as restrictions on voting that left the black population economically and politically powerless.

"We hold these truths to be self evident: that all men are created equal."

These words from the Declaration of Independence are the foundation of the civil rights movement in America. They promise equal treatment for all people. For some Americans, however, equality was denied—it had to be fought for by citizens uniting in support of peaceful change.

Bibliographical Note

History of the Civil Rights Movement Coloring Book is a new work, first published by Dover Publications, Inc., in 2010.

International Standard Book Number

ISBN-13: 978-0-486-47846-3
ISBN-10: 0-486-47846-7

Manufactured in the United States by Courier Corporation
47846701
www.doverpublications.com

On January 1, 1863, President Abraham Lincoln's Emancipation Proclamation freed the slaves in southern states that had refused to join the Union. The Thirteenth, Fourteenth, and Fifteenth Amendments to the Constitution granted full and equal rights to all citizens. Now those principles had to be enforced.

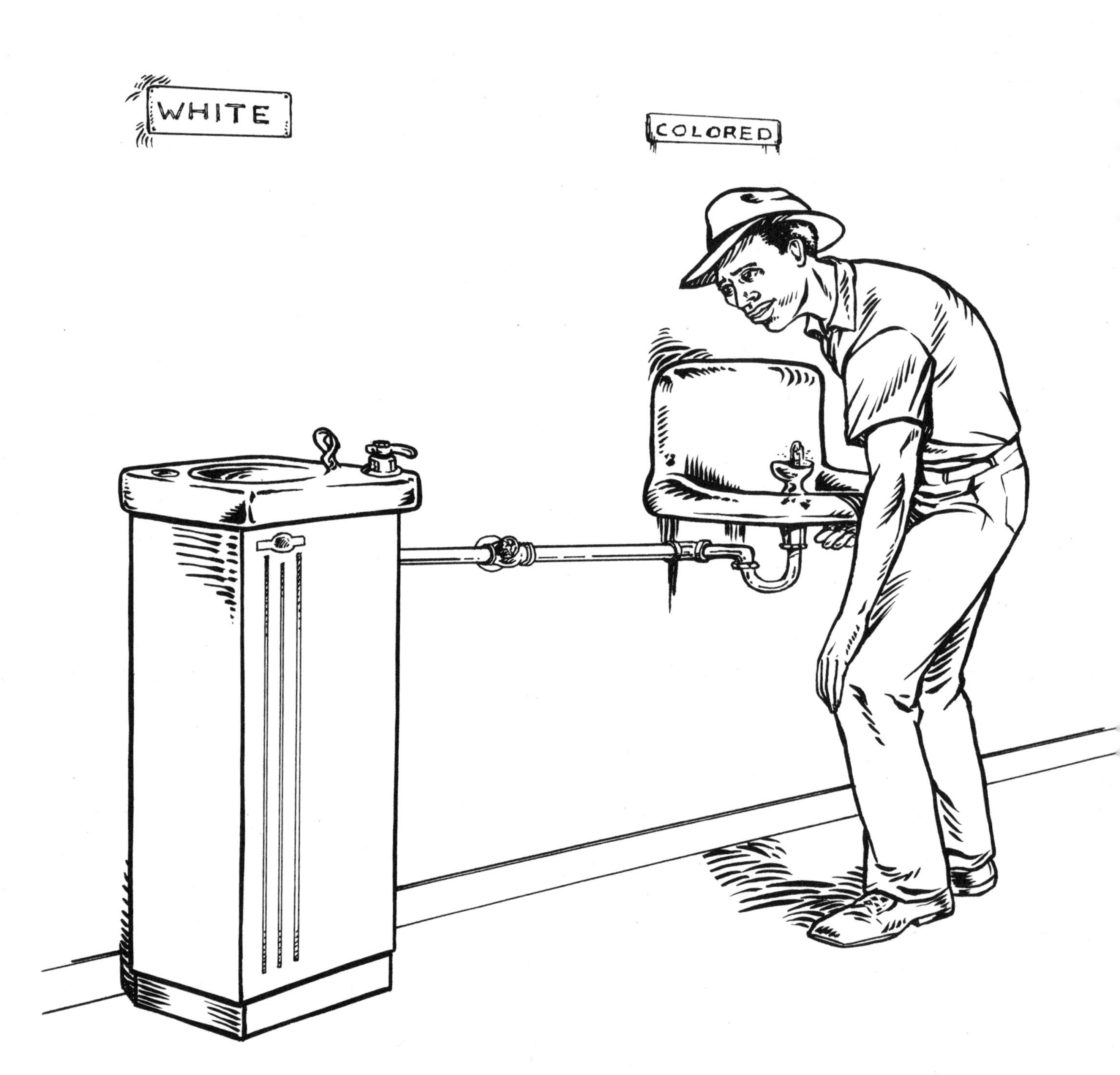

By 1880, "Jim Crow" codes, which resulted in "separate but equal" treatment for blacks, were in effect in parts of the United States. Separate facilities for African-American and white citizens, including schools, were not considered unequal by the courts. Segregation—separation on the basis of race in this case—was legal.

The NAACP—National Association for the Advancement of Colored People—was founded in 1909; it launched the effort to educate people that the practice of "separate but equal" was unjust, especially when it came to education. It was not until May 17, 1954, when NAACP attorney Thurgood Marshall won the case Brown v. the Board of Education of Topeka, Kansas, that the civil rights movement gained momentum. The outcome of the case: The Supreme Court ruled that separate educational facilities are basically unequal.

On December 1, 1955, in Montgomery, Alabama, Rosa Parks refused to give up her seat in the front of the "colored" section of a city bus to a white man. Her action led to a nearly yearlong bus boycott, led by the Reverend Martin Luther King, Jr., president of the Montgomery Improvement Association (MIA), and Ralph Abernathy, the MIA's vice president. The buses were desegregated in December 1956.

Martin Luther King, Jr., Charles K. Steele, and Fred L. Shuttlesworth founded the Southern Christian Leadership Conference in January 1956. The SCLC, based on the principles of nonviolence and civil disobedience, became a major force in organizing the civil rights movement.

In September 1957, the governor of Arkansas ordered the National Guard to block nine black students from entering Central High School in Little Rock. These students wanted the same education offered to whites.

President Dwight Eisenhower sent federal troops to Arkansas to protect the students, who became known as the "Little Rock Nine." The Civil Rights Act of 1957 was later passed, and a commission was formed to study the unfair treatment of blacks.

Four black students from North Carolina Agricultural and Technical College were refused service at a segregated Woolworth's lunch counter in Greensboro, North Carolina, in February 1960. They began a sit-in—a protest during which those involved in the sit-in refuse to move. Student sit-ins were increasingly effective ways of integrating parks, swimming pools, theaters, libraries, and other public places in the South.

In May 1961, the Congress of Racial Equality (CORE) sponsored activist groups known as "Freedom Riders." They traveled throughout the South to see whether laws that prohibited segregation on travel facilities were being enforced. Angry mobs attacked the Freedom Riders along the way.

The Reverend Martin Luther King, Jr. was arrested and jailed on April 16, 1963, during anti-segregation protests in Birmingham, Alabama. While in prison, he wrote his "Letter from Birmingham Jail," in which he states, ". . . freedom is never voluntarily given . . . it must be demanded." Dr. King believed that people have a moral duty to disobey unjust laws.

In 1963, President John F. Kennedy spoke about civil rights in a televised speech. He asked Congress to strengthen voting rights, create job opportunities for black people, and enforce school desegregation.

Civil rights protests became violent at times. In Birmingham, Alabama, Eugene "Bull" Connor, the commissioner of public safety, ordered his men to turn dogs and fire hoses on black demonstrators.

Images of these events were televised and seen all over the world, causing more people to support the civil rights movement.

Perhaps the greatest show of support for the civil rights movement occurred on August 28, 1963. The "March On Washington [for Jobs and Freedom]" brought over 200,000 people to the Lincoln Memorial in Washington, D.C. The crowds listened as the Reverend Martin Luther King, Jr. delivered his now-famous "I Have A Dream" speech.

On September 15, 1963, a bomb exploded at the 16th Street Baptist Church, a popular location for civil rights meetings in Birmingham, Alabama. Four young girls were killed in the bombing. Riots occurred afterwards, and the civil rights movement was tinged with violence.

Difficult literacy tests and polling taxes (a tax directed at black voters that was considered to be discriminatory) prevented many African Americans from voting in the South. In June 1964, civil rights organizations came together, along with many white college students, doctors, and lawyers from the North, to register as many black voters as possible. The Mississippi Summer Project—or Freedom Summer—was opposed by many white residents.

On July 2, 1965, President Lyndon Johnson signed the Civil Rights Act of 1964, which prohibits discrimination in public accommodations, in employment, and in any programs, educational or social, based on race, color, religion, or national origin. Yet violent acts continued, and in August three civil rights workers, James E. Chaney, Andrew Goodman, and Michael Schwerner, who were investigating the burning of a Mississippi church, were killed by Ku Klux Klan members.

Malcolm X, the black nationalist and founder of the Organization of Afro-American Unity, was shot to death on February 21, 1965, by members of the Black Muslim faith, which Malcolm had recently abandoned in favor of orthodox Islam. Malcolm resisted the mainstream civil rights movement, preferring instead to address issues of black identity in America.

Civil rights activists began a march from Selma, Alabama, to Montgomery on March 7, 1965, in support of voting rights.

Police used tear gas, whips, and clubs to stop them, and this event became known as Bloody Sunday. The Voting Rights Act was passed in response to the march.

On August 11, 1965, five days after the passage of the Voting Rights Act, which lifted rules that restricted black voter registration, riots broke out in the neighborhood of Watts in Los Angeles, California. The riots lasted for six days, and thirty-four people died. In September 1965, President Lyndon Johnson issued an Executive Order that required businesses working with the government to take "affirmative action" in hiring minority employees.

In 1966, offshoots of the civil rights movement became increasingly militant. The Black Panther Party was formed; it became known for its clashes with police. The party echoed the call for "black power" begun by Stokely Carmichael, a leader of SNCC (Student Nonviolent Coordinating Committee).

In 1967, Thurgood Marshall became the first African-American Supreme Court justice. Also in that year, Edward W. Brooke was elected senator from Massachusetts. He was the first African-American U.S. senator since the post-Civil War Reconstruction period.

On April 4, 1968, Reverend Martin Luther King, Jr. was in Memphis, Tennessee, to take part in a strike by black city workers. While standing on the balcony of his hotel, he was shot by a sniper. Dr. King was thirty-nine years old. His assassination sparked riots throughout the country. President Lyndon Johnson declared a national day of mourning soon after.

The U.S. Supreme Court ruled in favor of busing as a means of desegregating public schools on April 20, 1971. The decision was expected to assure that schools would be fairly integrated, enabling all students to receive equal educational opportunities, regardless of their race.

In December 1971, Reverend Jesse Jackson, an organizer for the SCLC (Southern Christian Leadership Conference) founded Operation PUSH—People United to Serve Humanity. His goal was to give disadvantaged Americans, including people of color, more opportunities in jobs and education.

In 1984, Jesse Jackson became the first African-American man to make a serious bid for the U.S. presidency by campaigning for the Democratic Party nomination. Although unsuccessful, he made a second attempt in 1988.

In 1986, legislation (signed earlier by President Ronald Reagan) established Martin Luther King, Jr.'s birthday as a national holiday. The holiday occurs on the third Monday in January each year. It commemorates the work of Dr. King, as well as symbolizing a day of service to others.